Afi
and the magic drum
A story from Benin

Written by Thécla Midiohouan
Illustrations by Hector Sonon

(in collaboration with the Bénin National Reading Campaign)

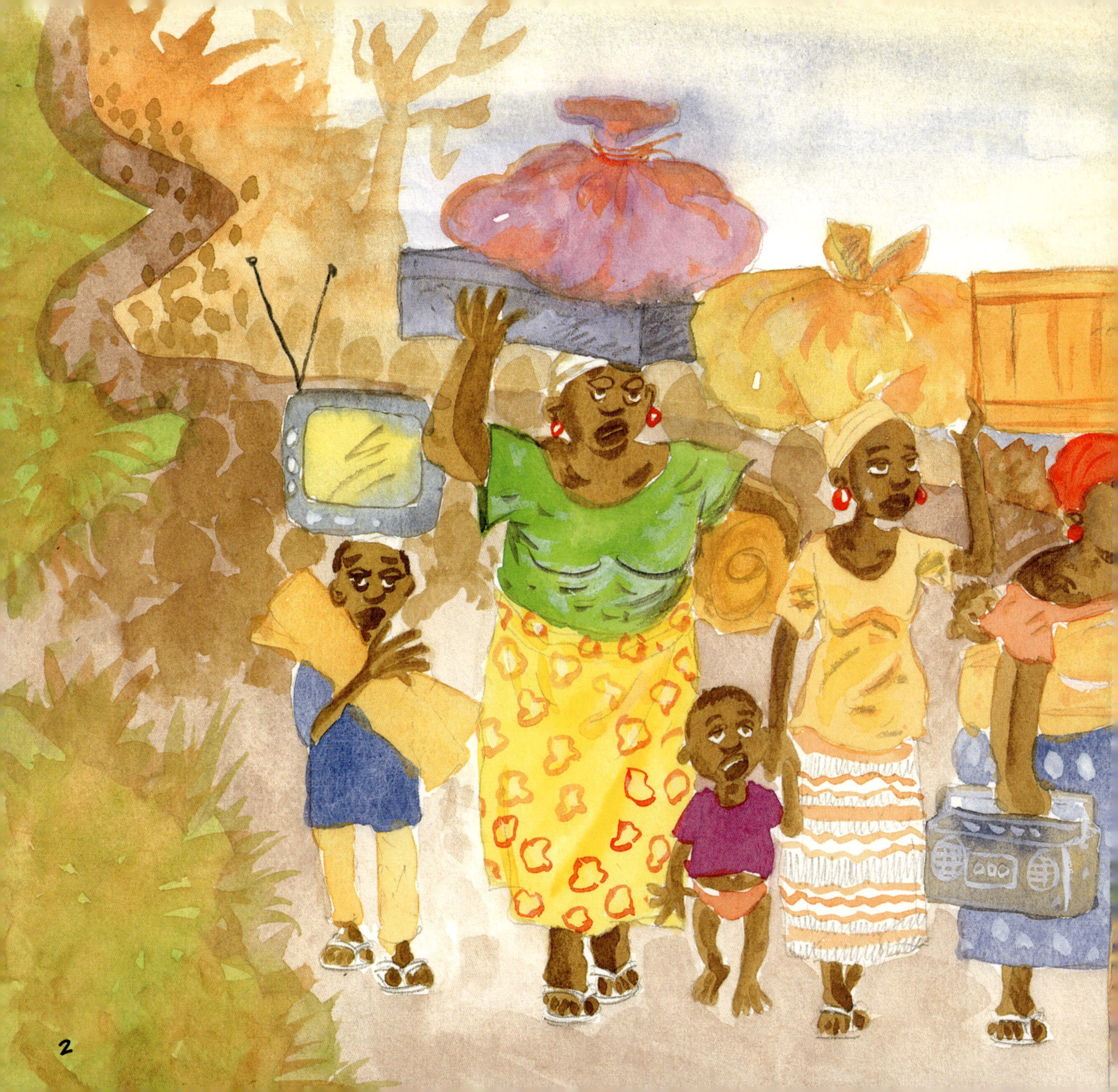

One day a war broke out in Afi's country. She and her parents fled from their village, in search of a safe place to stay. In the crowd, Afi got lost. She could not find her parents.

"Where are they? Which road have they taken?" she asked herself.

Afi was alone. She started crying. She cried all day and all night. Her eyes were so filled with tears that she could no longer see.

4

Afi walked all on her own for a long time. Eventually she was so tired that she lay down next to the road and fell fast asleep.

The owls in the forest were the only creatures watching over her while she slept.

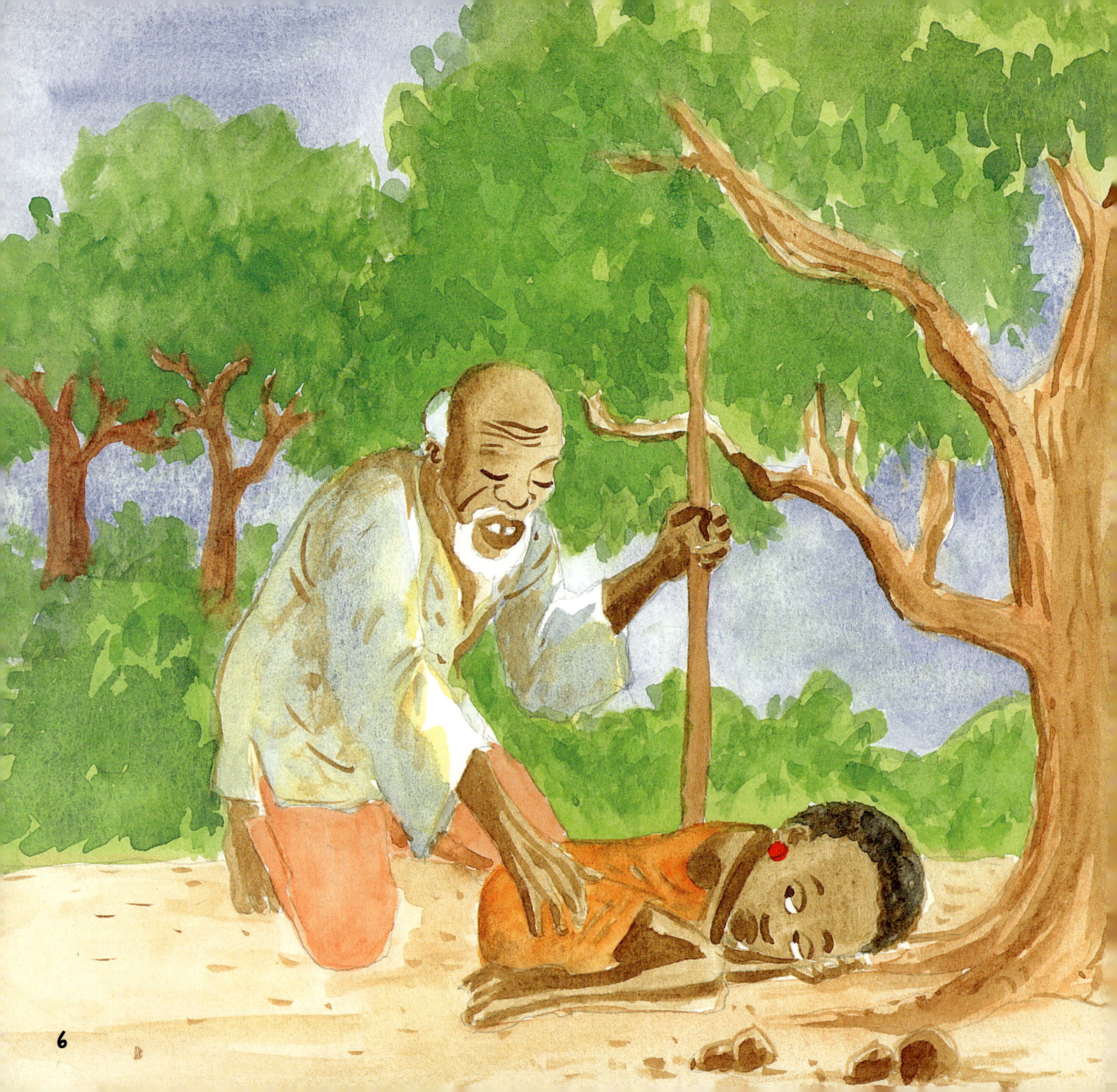

Afi woke up. An old man was shaking her.

"Wake up, little girl," he said. "What is a little girl doing out here all by herself? She must be hungry. Hey! Little girl, get up and come with me."

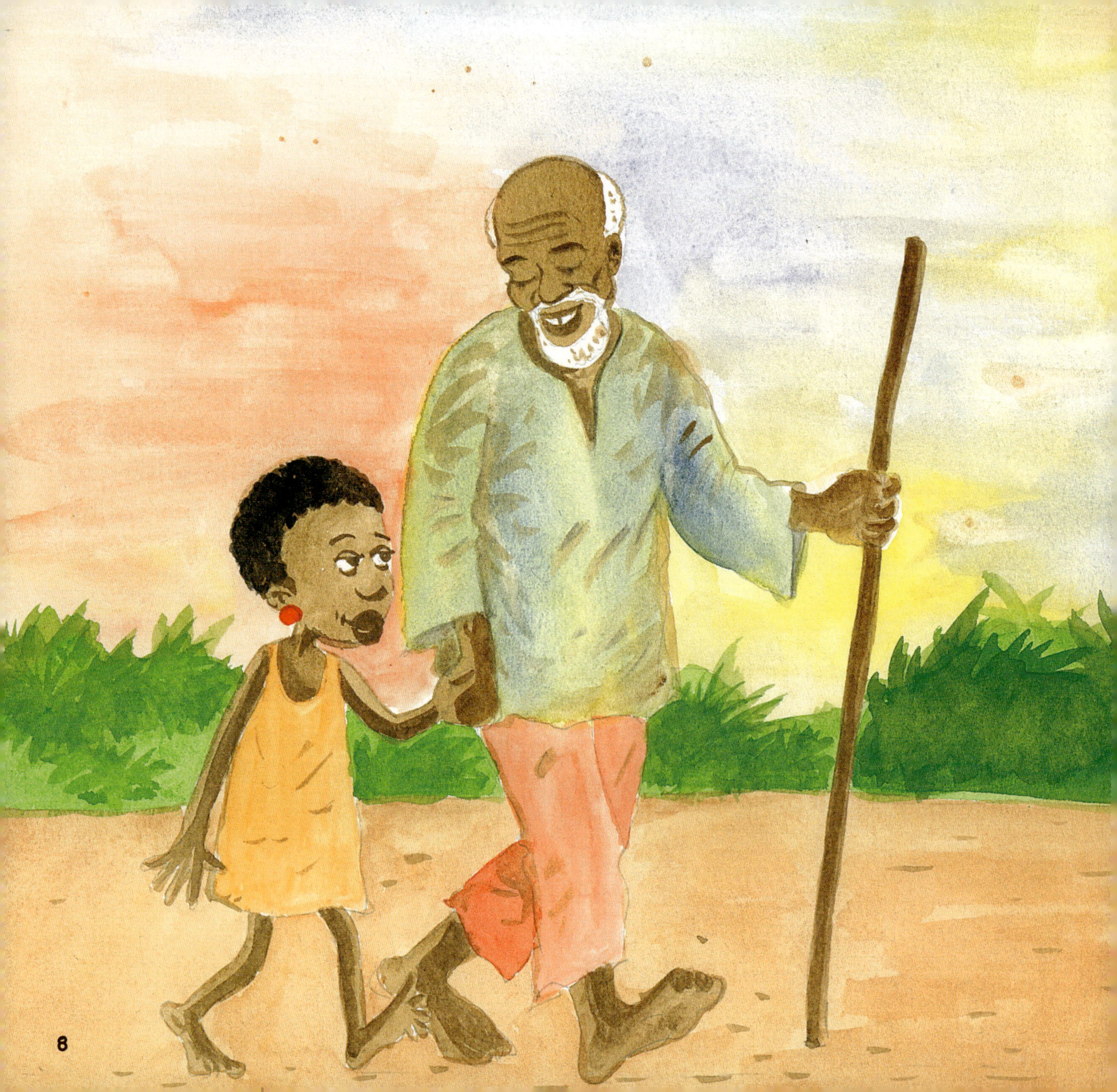

Afi set off with the old man.

"What luck, someone to speak to!" Afi thought. "It doesn't matter that he is old and a little dirty."

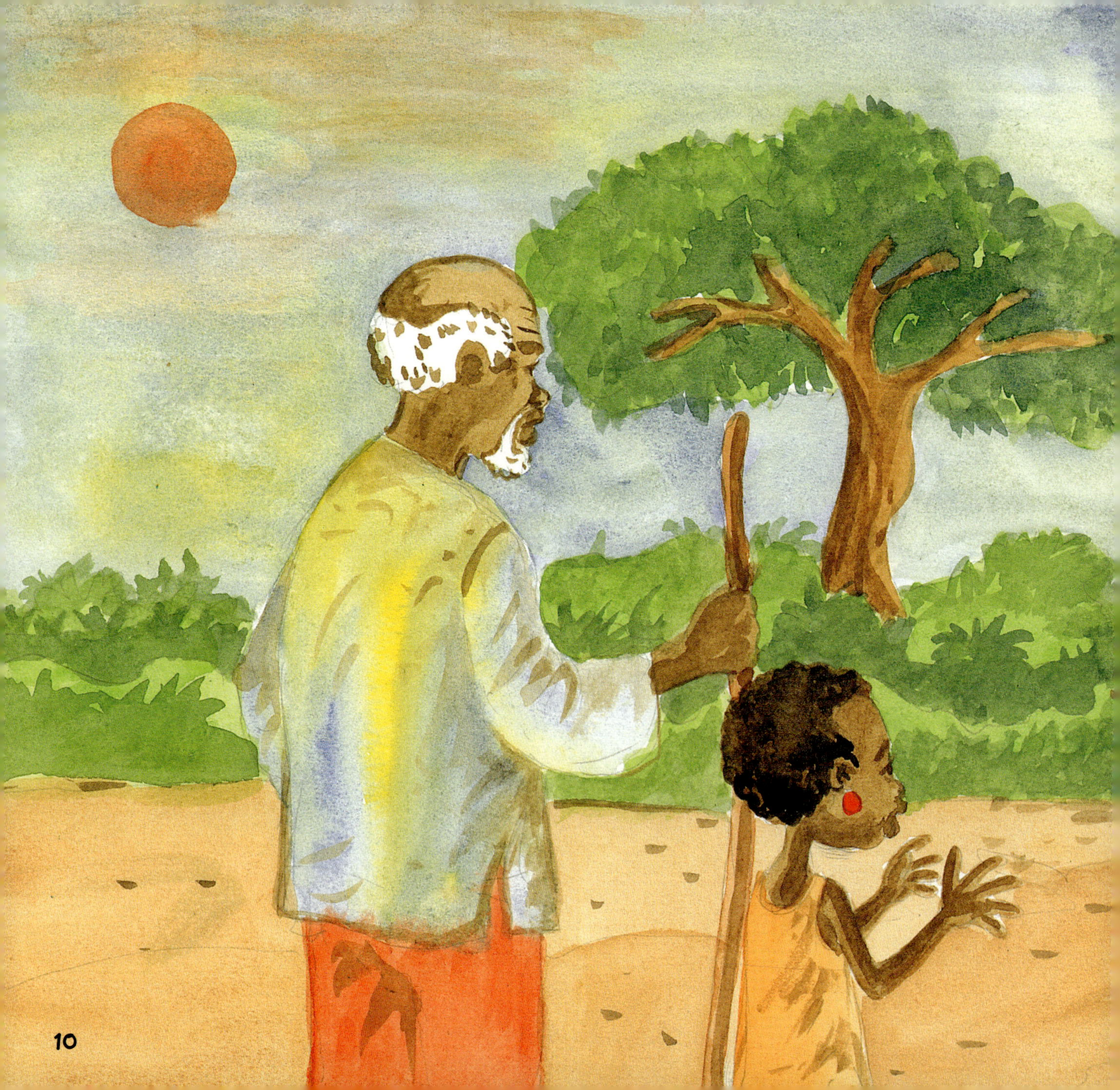

They finally got to an old tumbledown hut.
This was where the old man lived.

12

Afi was glad to help the old man.
She ground some grain and cooked a meal.
She fetched water from the river to fill the
water pot and the big jars. She swept the
hut and cleaned the dishes.

Afi had found a place she could call home. She lived there with the old man for a long time. Every evening, the old man told her wonderful stories. One of the stories was about an elephant that lost its trunk. There was another story about a monkey that ate too many bananas. Afi loved to sit and listen for hours.

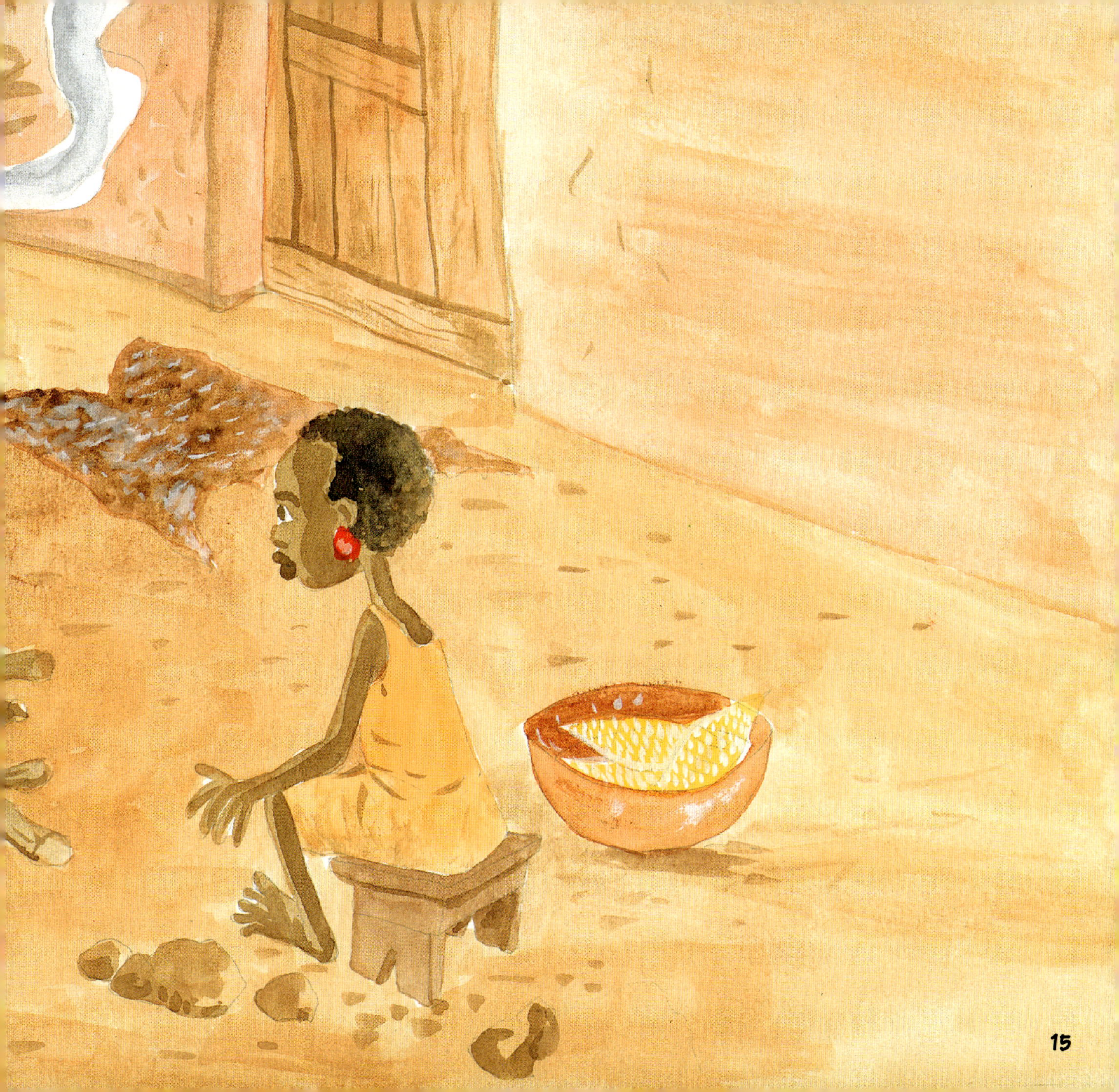

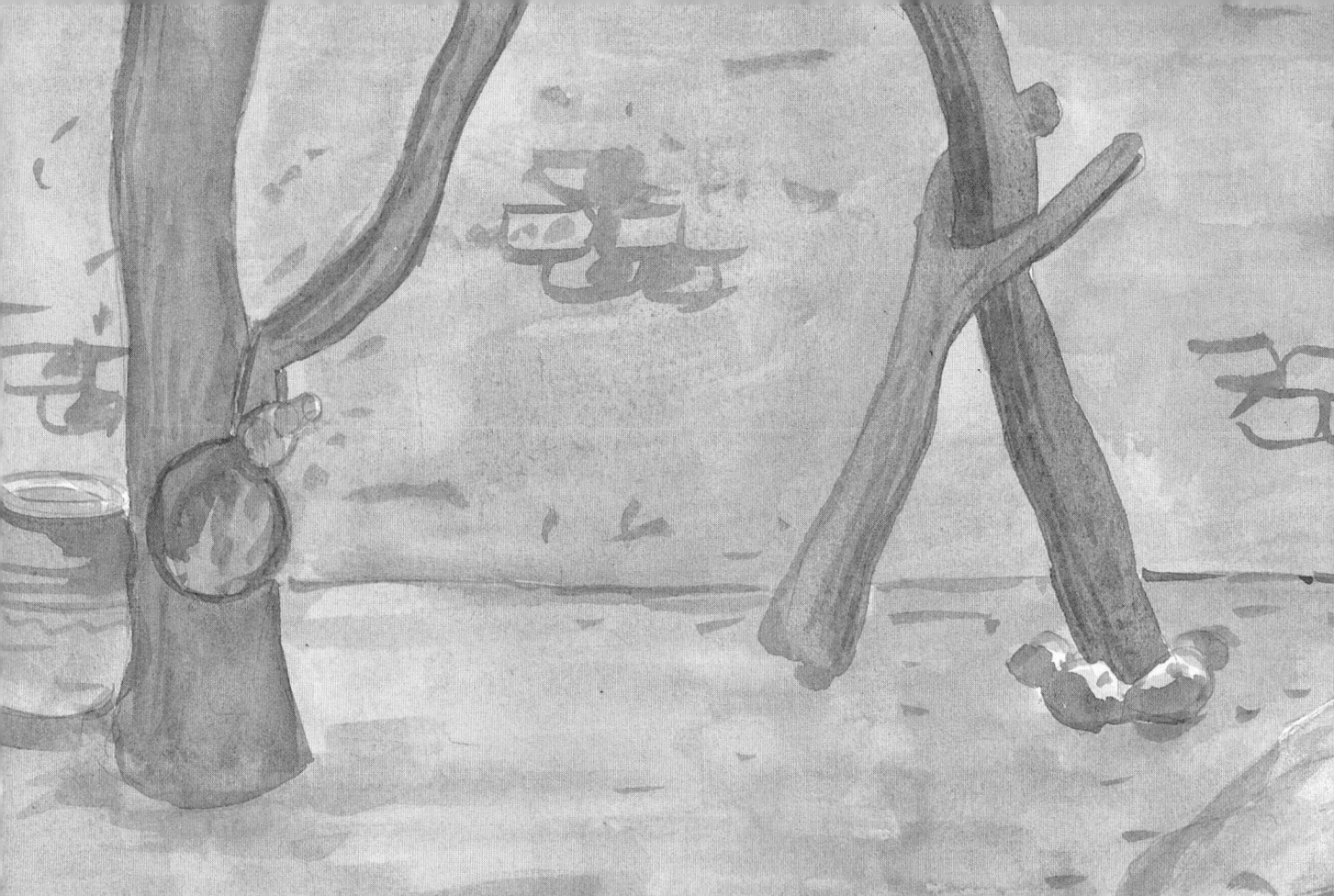

One day, the old man fell ill. He knew that he would die soon. He called Afi and said to her, "I want to give you a gift before I go to a faraway place. Take this little drum. Whenever you get to a crossroad, beat on it three times."

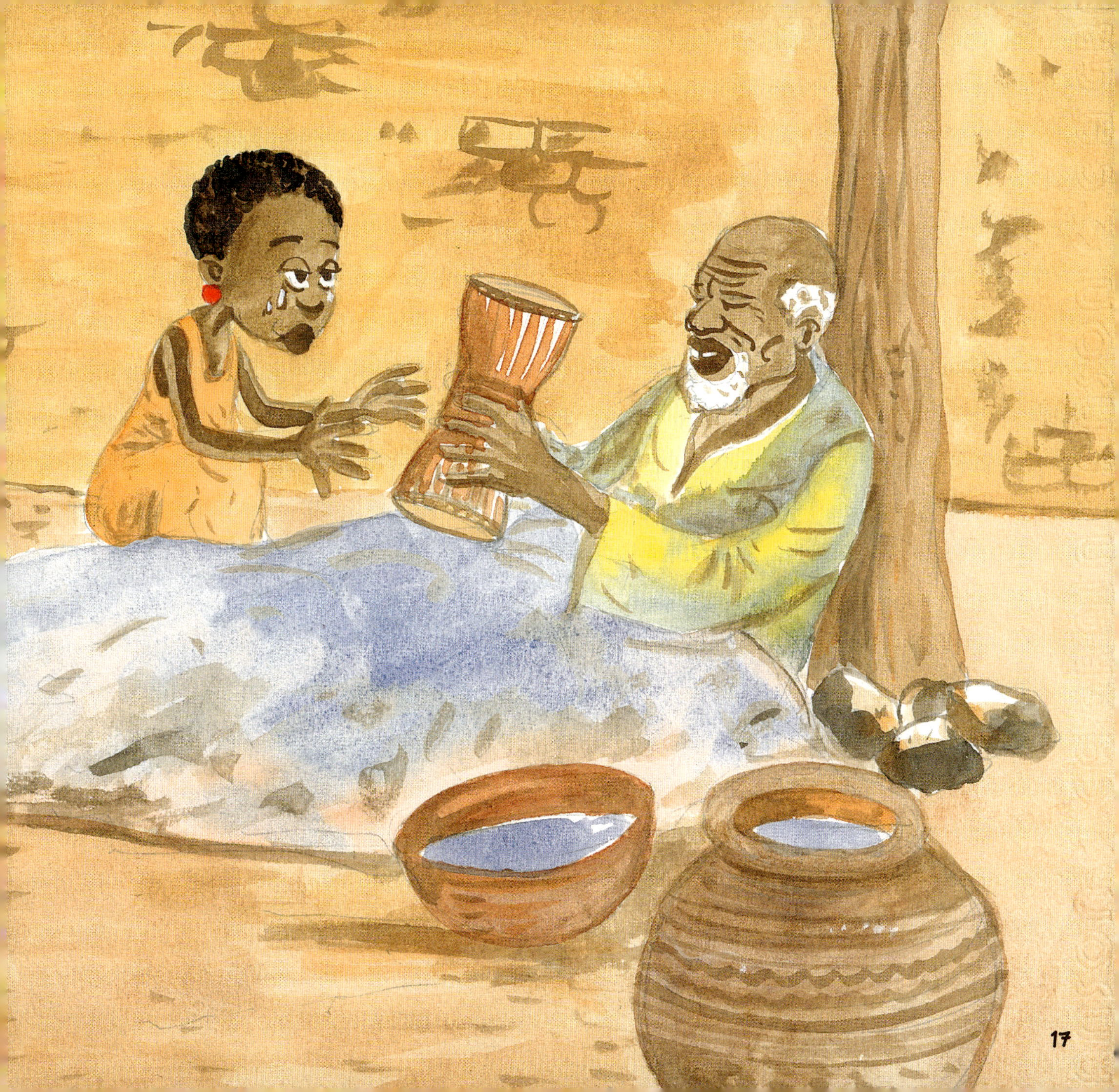

Afi was very sad. She had lost her friend. What would happen to her now?

She left the old man's hut. She walked for a long, long time, until she got to a crossroad. She remembered what the old man had told her and she beat the drum three times: *tam, tam, tam*!

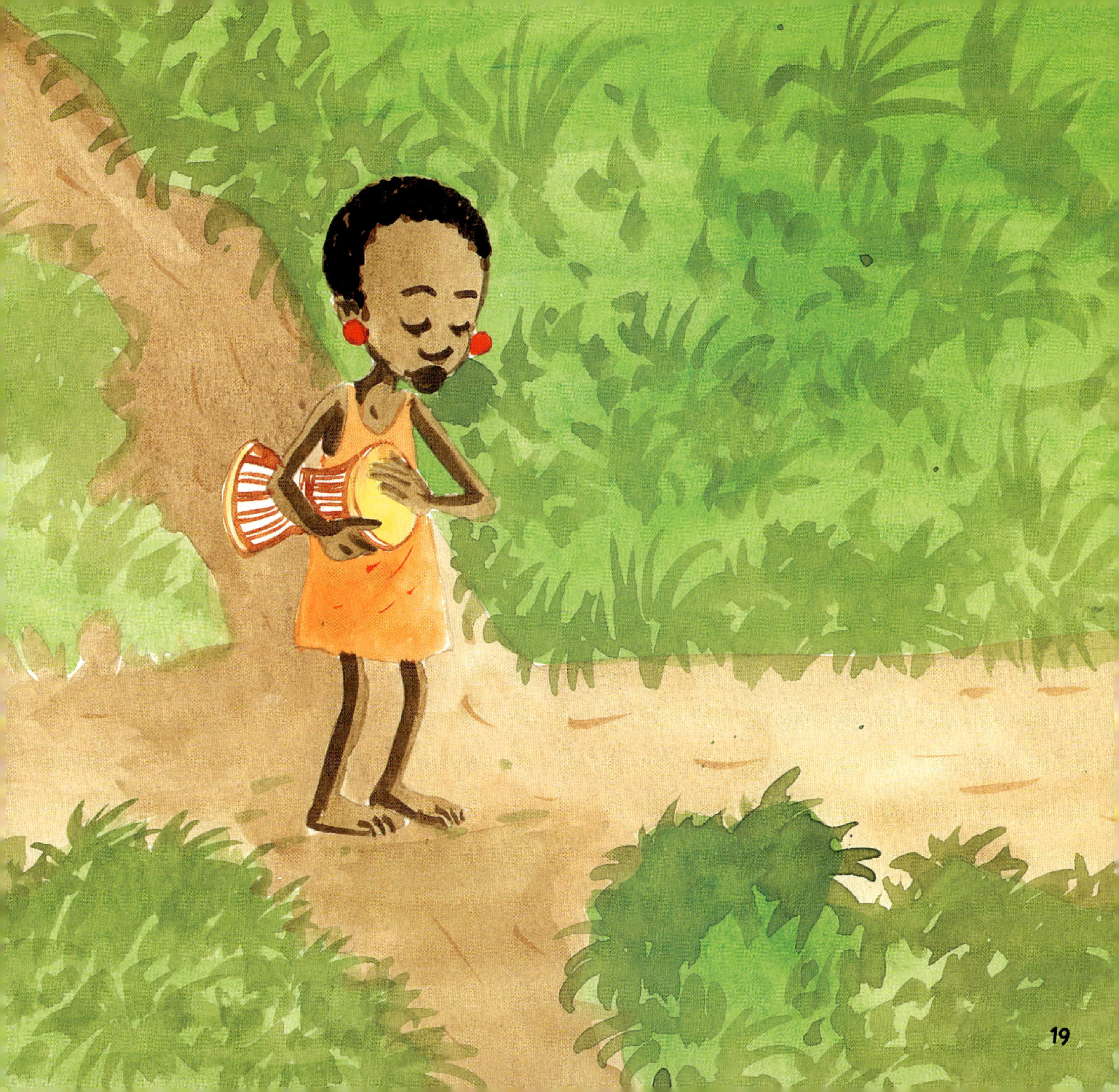

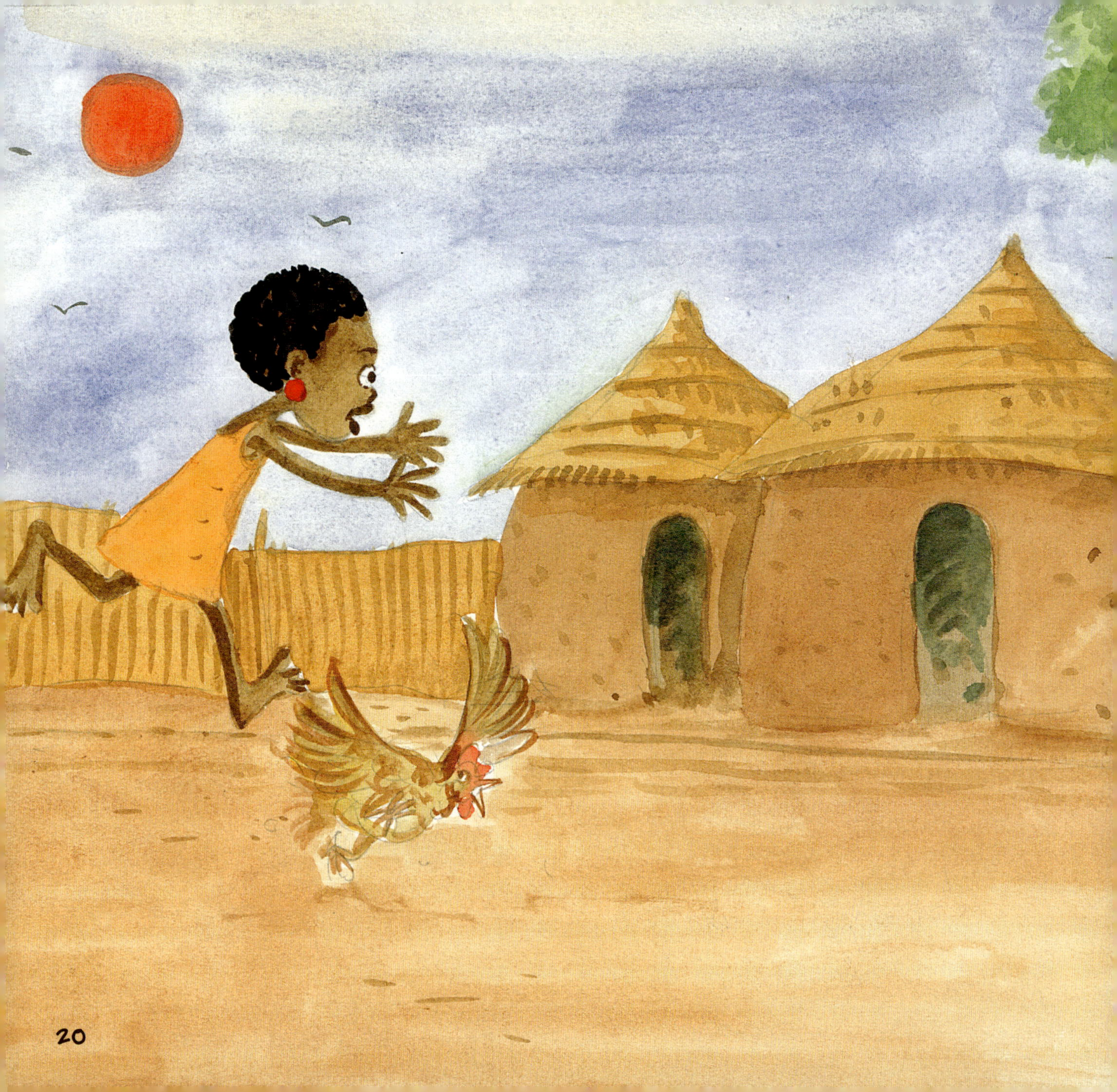

It was magic! Afi found herself back in her old village! The trees had grown taller. The huts had been rebuilt. Afi ran towards the compound where her parents lived. "Daddy, Mummy, there you are!"

She jumped into their arms.

23